Pandora's Box

Written by Julia Golding

Illustrated by J. Solomon

Essex County Council

3013021280637 5

Chapter 1

I opened my eyes. A bright blue sky stretched overhead.

"Come, Father!" called a gruff voice. "She's finished."

I turned my head. I was lying on a worktable with a pillow under my neck. Someone stood nearby at a workbench holding a hammer. He was beating out stars on his anvil, and sparks were flying in brilliant showers before dying on the floor.

"Where am I?" I asked.

"Hello, my lovely creation," the craftsman smiled.
He dipped a star in a bucket of cold water, releasing
a hiss of steam. "You're on Mount Olympus, home of
the gods."

"Are you a god then?" I sat up, surprised at how strong
I felt. I felt as though I could run and run and never stop.

He threw the star up into the sky where it vanished with a wink of light. "Yes. My name's Hephaestus, god of all who make things."

"What kind of things?" I asked.

"I made you, for one," Hephaestus replied.

"Me?" I touched my chest, and then stared at my fingers. I'd light brown skin, small hands and fingernails shaped like almonds. I realised that I'd never seen them before. Everything about me was new.

"Yes. You were a special order from my father."

"Why?" I spread my fingers; then closed them tight. Everything was in working order.

"He asked me to make you as a gift to mankind," replied Hephaestus.

Puzzled, I slid down from the table and stood in front of a polished shield to look at my reflection. My hair was the colour of an acorn and my eyes were bright green like new leaves. "How did you know to make me look like this?"

Hephaestus chuckled. "I modelled you on my wife, Aphrodite, the goddess of love."

A second god strode into the workshop. I knew at once from the way the air shimmered around him that this one was even more powerful.

"Is she finished?" His voice rang through my body, making my bones hum.

"Yes, Father," said Hephaestus.

The god turned to me and smiled. His teeth were so white I had to shade my eyes. I hadn't feared Hephaestus, but something about this god scared me.

"I'm Zeus, ruler of Olympus."

I sank to my knees and bowed my head. I thought it wise to show respect to such a powerful being.

"I've a very important job for you. I want you to learn everything the gods have to teach you. Then you'll go to Earth and marry a man that I've chosen for you. He's called Epimetheus," Zeus ordered.

"Yes, Zeus," I answered. I'd so many questions – I wanted to know more about the man I was to marry on Earth – but I'd quickly understood that I should obey and not question Zeus.

"Come with me. You'll begin your lessons immediately," Zeus commanded.

I had to run to keep up with the mighty Zeus.

Chapter 2

First, he introduced me to Athena, his beloved daughter, the goddess of wisdom. She was very beautiful, with grey eyes and soft brown hair. Owls surrounded her weaving loom, hooting for her delight as she expertly used the shuttle.

"Athena, you know what you're to do?" asked Zeus.

"Yes, Father: teach her the skills she needs to know on Earth." Athena smiled at me. "We'll start with weaving."

"Good. Return her to me when her education's complete," Zeus ordered.

When Zeus left us, I bowed to Athena. "It's kind of you to take the time to teach me these skills. Thank you."

"Kind?" The goddess smiled a secret kind of smile. "I wouldn't call it kind. You've become part of a much larger plan my father has designed. I think it's rather a pity myself."

Confused, I looked at Athena urging her to explain what she meant by this.

She gestured to the cloth she was weaving. Studying it spread out before me, I quickly decided that I didn't like the picture. It showed a man chained to a rock, his stomach being pecked at by a giant vulture. He was clearly in agony.

"What does this mean?" I asked.

"This man's the brother of your future husband. Prometheus is his name. He made the mistake of disobeying my father. He stole fire from the gods and gave it to man, even though Zeus had forbidden it. Men went from being simple creatures unable to make weapons, to becoming beings armed with swords made in the fires of their workshops. One day, they may rival us gods."

I frowned, trying to make sense of this. "Surely no one could be more powerful than Zeus?"

"Nothing, not even a god's power, lasts for ever," Athena replied. She cut the threads binding the cloth to the loom, folded it and put it out of sight. "Come with me, I'll teach you how to make clothes."

I followed Athena, barely hiding my frustration. I was rapidly learning that the gods never tell you everything you want to know.

When it came to skills, however, Athena was a kind and patient teacher. I watched in awe, paying careful attention to everything she taught me.

When I'd mastered weaving, Athena gave me a beautiful dress she'd made from the the most luxurious material. She draped gold necklaces around me and put a chain of white flowers in my hair.

"These flowers will never fade, because they come from Olympus," she told me. "Now, come: I'll introduce you to my brother, Hermes, messenger of the gods."

Chapter 3

Athena sent an owl to summon Hermes. He arrived in a flash of silver light. He was a tall, athletic young man.

"Sister, what do you want?" he asked.

"Hermes, Father wants you to teach my pupil how to be clever with her words," Athena replied.

Hermes looked at me and held out his hand. "The best way to learn such things is to see for yourself," he said. "So, are you ready?"

Wondering what was going to happen, I nodded and tentatively put my hand in his. My heart was beating fast. I didn't know what to expect. Then ... Olympus rushed away – or so it seemed. In reality, it was Hermes and I who were moving close to the speed of light. Suddenly, we dropped down among mankind. They couldn't see us but we could see them.

Hermes showed me arguments and agreements, deals
and threats. After each conversation that we listened
to, he'd praise a clever speaker or point out someone
who was too blunt in the way they tried to get their way.
By the time we'd gone round the whole world, I'd had
a complete education in all the right and wrong ways to
use speech.

We landed back in Olympus at sunset. The trees turned golden in the fading light and bright stars popped out from their hiding places.

Hermes ruffled my hair. "You're a good student, youngster. I could see you were listening and learning."

"A student's only as good as their teacher, and I had the best," I said politely.

He grinned. "See, you've already learnt to flatter. Your last lesson is one that I can't teach. I'm leaving you with Aphrodite, the goddess of love. Go into her grove."

21

Chapter 4

I followed a silvery path into the grove of
rustling trees. Their leaves danced like the sparks
in Hephaestus's workshop. The air was thick with
the sweet scent of flowers and spices. The goddess was
lying by a pool in the middle of the grove, trailing her
delicate hand in the clear water. She lifted her sparkling
sea-green eyes when she heard me approach.

"Your majesty, Hermes sent me." I bowed low.

Aphrodite looked at me and laughed. "My goodness, it's like looking in a mirror. Who's this gorgeous creature?" Her laughter was like the tinkle of a fountain, falling cool and sweet upon the listener's ears. Once you heard it, you couldn't get enough of it. "Oh, silly me, I remember. My husband made you to look like me."

Remembering my lessons with Hermes, I knew this was a time to flatter. "Hephaestus, greatest of craftsmen, wanted to mirror the very best that he knew."

"True." She smiled and patted the grass beside her. "Zeus said to tell you how to make people love you. That's simple, all you have to do is do as I do."

"And what do you do?" I asked.

"I'm always and only myself. I never listen to the opinions of others. I act as I want to act. That's the secret of being loved," Aphrodite replied.

She seemed such a proud and powerful goddess, I felt a little jealous. Could I ever make myself loved as she'd done? I decided to pay careful attention to her to learn her secrets.

I spent the night sitting at her feet, listening to stories of those who'd come and gone in her life. Listening to her words, I learnt the lessons she had to teach. But was there something missing? I wondered. She never seemed very happy with any of her relationships, nor did the people who loved her. But I kept that thought to myself as Hermes had taught me never to criticise someone so much more powerful than me.

Chapter 5

As the sun rose, all my teachers gathered in
Aphrodite's grove to take me to Zeus.
They led me to the throne room where
he sat watching the world wake
up to a new day.

"We've taught her all
she needs to know,"
said Athena.
"She's ready."

Zeus tapped his fingers on the arm of his throne. Little rumbles of thunder echoed in the skies. "Good. Then I'll name her. You're Pandora, which means one to whom all gifts have been given."

I bowed, astonished by his generosity. "Thank you, sir."

"Before you go to your new husband, I've a special gift for you." He waved his hand and a small box appeared before him. The box was as black as night, and decorated in white with scenes from many of the stories I'd heard. "Take this box. It's a wedding gift. But listen carefully: you must never open it."

I picked up the box. It felt much heavier than it looked and I could hear intriguing noises coming from inside it. I itched to open it but I knew better than to disobey Zeus, at least while he was watching. "Thank you, sir. I'll treasure it."

"Now, let me introduce you to your husband."
With that, Zeus and I had left Olympus and
were standing on the veranda of a fine house by
the shores of the Mediterranean. We interrupted
a young man with curly brown hair in the middle
of his breakfast. He dropped the roll he'd been
eating and lay flat on the floor.

"Epimetheus?" boomed Zeus.

"Zeus?" The man lifted his head a fraction; his body was trembling.

"Arise, don't be afraid. I'm going to reward you to balance the punishment your brother Prometheus suffers." Zeus waved me forward. "See, I've made a companion for you, a new creature called a woman. Isn't that kind of me?"

I found myself blushing as Epimetheus looked at me in amazement.

"My brother stole fire from you, Sir, and went against your orders, and yet you give me this great gift? How ever can I thank you?" asked my new husband.

"By accepting her and that box she carries as her wedding present. Her name's Pandora. She comes with the blessing of all the gods." Zeus smiled and lightning flashed. "But there's one condition. That box she holds must only be admired and never opened. Do you understand?"

33

"Yes, sir. I'll put it in a place of honour in my house so everyone may see how beautiful it is, but not touch it."

Zeus nodded. "Then all will be well. I'll leave you two to get to know each other."

With that Zeus left, taking half the air and all of the light out of the room with him.

I looked at my new husband and saw that he, like me, was astonished by the comings and goings of the gods. Despite being strangers, at least that gave us something in common. I hoped that we could become good friends over time.

Chapter 6

Epimetheus was a very kind man. When we met at meal times, he spoke to me gently and made me laugh with his jokes. He made sure my room was comfortable and I'd everything I needed to carry on with my weaving. With a large farm to look after, he passed his days tending to his animals in the fields.

His friends and neighbours came to visit, all marvelling over me as they'd never seen a woman before. Everyone was kind and welcoming, but still I felt alone.

Thanks to Athena's lessons, I'd everything running smoothly within a few days. In fact, there wasn't enough to do. With Epimetheus out with his flocks and his horses, I soon grew bored and lonely. The room in which the whispering box was displayed drew me back time after time. I'd sit with my ear pressed against it, trying to work out what it was telling me.

One night at supper, I asked Epimetheus if we could take just a little peek inside. "I think there's something trapped," I explained softly. "I'm worried it might need more air."

Epimetheus stood up and pushed away from the table. "No, Pandora. You aren't to touch it. Zeus must be obeyed."

I thought of Epimetheus's brother, Prometheus, who'd stolen fire for us humans, allowing us to eat cooked food and use tools made from metal. Without him, we'd be little better than my husband's sheep. Surely he'd been right not to obey Zeus?

I watched Epimetheus stride out to say goodnight to his horses, and felt angry that he hadn't listened.

The next day, Epimetheus went out early again. I didn't mean to go back and yet I still found myself heading towards the room that held my box. The curiosity was killing me. I had to see what was in that container. Aphrodite had told me that the secret to being loved was to do whatever you liked. It was time I put that to the test.

39

The black box sat on its pedestal, looming over me like the vulture in the picture on Athena's loom. I hesitated with my hand over the lid. The whispering from inside sounded more like music today, beautiful songs of the gods. My mind made up, I lifted the lid.

Whoosh! The white room filled with black smoke. In the choking fumes, voices screamed and wailed.

"I'm sickness!" screeched one, slipping out under the door.

"I'm hunger!" cried another.

"I bring despair and disaster!" wailed a third.

"Hard work for no reward!" shrieked the next.

"Sadness is mine!"

The smoke brushed past me, stinging my eyes. Panicking, I fumbled to close the lid, but the bad things just kept on pouring out of the box.

Anger flared inside me. I knew then that Zeus had tricked me. He'd always meant me to open the box. When Hephaestus had made me, he'd given me a double dose of curiosity and little caution. Zeus had sent me to punish mankind for the fire that Prometheus had stolen for them.

I understood now what Athena had meant when she said I was part of a much larger plan. I was angry at the gods for lying to me, and at my husband for not being there, but mostly I was angry with myself for falling into the trap that Zeus had set.

But I couldn't blame the gods now. It was my job to stop more terrible things escaping into the world. Standing on tiptoes, I eventually forced the lid closed and the smoke cleared. From beyond the window, I could see the blue sky clouding over, a storm coming and the crops being beaten down by hail.

"So it begins," I whispered. I hugged the box and wept. As my tears trickled over the smooth black surface, I could hear a little voice inside the container. I pressed my ear against the cool surface. "Who's there?" I asked.

"Hope," came the answer. "Everyone has left but me. I'll stay with you and all humans, helping you to cope with the bad things that've just escaped as the gods planned."

"Hope?" I kissed the box. "Thank you for staying with me. We're going to need you."

Dear Diary

That box is haunting me. It's sitting on
a special stand not far from where I'm writing.
My husband's told me not to touch it, but I
think there must be something trapped inside.
I can hear whispering and muttering when I go
near it, pulling me towards it. What could Zeus
have put in there? He's an all-powerful god so it
could be anything. Or maybe, as Epimetheus
says, it's nothing.

But I can't ignore the noise. I can't think of
anything else. I dream about the good that

the box could hold and, in my nightmares –
the bad ... I've shaken it but there's no rattling.
I've sniffed it, but other than a faint whiff of
flowers there's no scent. It's surprisingly light
for its size, just the right weight for me to lift
without any difficulty.

Should I open it and see? I could sneak in and
do it while Epimetheus is out. He doesn't need
to know. Surely nothing too bad could happen
as long as I just take a quick peek?

Oh, help me to decide.

Yours, Pandora

Ideas for reading

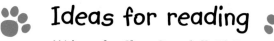

Written by Clare Dowdall, PhD
Lecturer and Primary Literacy Consultant

Reading objectives:
- identify themes and conventions in a wide range of books
- discuss words and phrases that capture the reader's interest and imagination
- identify main ideas drawn from more than one paragraph and summarise ideas

Spoken language objectives:
- use spoken language to develop understanding through speculating, hypothesising, imagining and exploring ideas

Curriculum links: History – ancient Greece and ancient Greek culture

Resources: thought bubble cards; ICT for research and presentation; boxes and art materials for junk modelling

Build a context for reading
- Ask children if they have ever been tempted to do something they've been forbidden to do. Discuss what resisting temptation feels like, and introduce this language.
- Look at the image on the front cover. Ask children to suggest what might be in Pandora's box.
- Read the blurb together. Check that children understand that this is a mythical story from ancient Greece. Check that children understand the term "mankind".

Understand and apply reading strategies
- Walk through Chapter 1 together to find the names of the characters in the story. Help children to pronounce them.
- Read Chapter 1, taking turns to read aloud. Ask children to pause when they notice vivid descriptions of the characters.